# ENGAGED BY CHRISTMAS

## MAIL ORDER BRIDES OF SHADOW GULCH

## SUSANNAH CALLOWAY

Tica House
Publishing

Sweet Romance that Delights and Enchants!

**Dearest Readers,**

Thank you so much for choosing one of my books. I am proud to be a part of the team of writers at Tica House Publishing who work joyfully to bring you stories of hope, faith, courage, and love. Your kind words and loving readership are deeply appreciated.

I would like to personally invite you to sign up for updates and to become part of our **Exclusive Reader Club**—it's completely Free to join! We'd love to welcome you!

**Much love,**

**Susannah Calloway**

**VISIT HERE to Join our Reader's Club and to Receive Tica House Updates!**

https://wesrom.subscribemenow.com/

# CONTENTS

# CHAPTER 1

November of 1873 had a biting wind that Elliot Sanders could not remember from any other year of his life in Shadow Gulch, Idaho. It did more than go right through the thick nap of his coat and flannels; it went right through him, chilling him to the bone. It was going to be a bad winter, he thought as he put another chunk of wood on the fire. If that wind was anything to go by, there would be more cases of influenza, more bad colds, more fevers than the little town of Shadow Gulch had seen in a long while.

Rubbing his hands together to warm them up a little, he returned to the second room in his office and mustered up a smile for Albert Cole, who sat on the examination table with his shoulders hunched.

"The good news, Al, is that you're going to live." He kept his tone jovial and light, letting the young man know he was joking with him. But Albert still was clearly feeling miserable and in no mood for jocularity. Elliot pulled up the stool and sat down near him with a sigh.

"When am I gonna feel better, Doc Sanders?"

"The fever is running its course. I know your ma was worried about you, but it's really just a relatively mild case of the influenza. You're young and strong and healthy – you'll feel better in a few days. Drink lots of fluids and keep the fire going in the house." He glanced out the tiny window at the back of the examination room. "Tell your pa I said that you're to be kept off chores until Saturday. That'll give you a little bit of recovery time without being too much of a hardship on the farm. You hear me, Al?"

"Yes, Doc."

"All right. That's just fine. Head on home now, son, and take care of yourself."

He put a gentle hand on the boy's shoulder and walked him back out and through the front door. It was rapidly growing dark, the change in the season meaning that the day ended several hours earlier than it did during the summer. Elliot wished devoutly that there were more hours in the day; he never seemed to get enough done.

But if there were more hours in the day, he reckoned, he might just keel over and die from exhaustion. Albert was only the last of the sixteen patients he had seen that day alone; some were more dire than others, of course, but all of them had a legitimate complaint, and all needed care. The life of a small-town doctor was certainly not glamorous, but it did make him feel needed…

His life at home made him feel needed, too, of course. Sometimes a bit too much. His niece Maria and the twins would be waiting for him, wondering what was keeping him, but knowing in their hearts he was incapable of turning away anyone who needed his help.

He extinguished the oil lamps, banked down the fire, and closed the door behind him firmly. The doctor's office was never locked. He kept the medicine cupboards locked up, of course, in the examination room, but in his opinion, if someone needed a warm place to shelter for the night, they were welcome to it. It felt like part of his responsibility to the town.

And Elliot Sanders always took his responsibilities very seriously.

Shadow Gulch wasn't his hometown, though it was now the town which he called home. He'd grown up several miles away to the east, in Verity, Idaho. But he'd been here for nearly six years now – in fact, he realized with a slight chill, it would be six years a month from today – and he had thrown his heart and soul into serving the town as though he'd been born and bred there.

Besides, Shadow Gulch had been good to him. The people were welcoming, the town itself neat and tidy for a place in the territories. It was as good a place as any to raise Maria, Mattie, and Martha, and better than some. He should just be grateful for what he had, not waste his time thinking on things he was lacking…or things that he had lost.

He shook the surge of memories from his head and trudged home, head down against the bitter wind.

Maria, bless her sweet and helpful heart, had supper waiting on the table for him. The twins, seven years old and rambunctious even at this late hour, were teasing and pinching each other, squirming on their chairs at the supper table. Maria took Elliot's coat and hat and shooed him toward the kitchen; he went, smiling.

"Maria, you're far too young to be this much of a mother," he told her. "I don't know what I'd do without you."

"Oh, it's nothing, Uncle Elliot. Just stew, for goodness' sake. Don't thank me before you eat it."

That made him laugh outright. At fifteen, Maria was a better cook than most grown women Elliot knew, and he had no idea how she had managed to develop the skill. She certainly hadn't had any feminine influence in the past six years, and the Lord knew he hadn't been any great shakes at preparing meals for the children. In fact, at nine, Maria had not only grasped his lack of expertise, she had tactfully stepped in one day when he was working late at his new office in Shadow Gulch, preparing not only supper but also thinking ahead and telling him cheerfully not to worry about breakfast the next morning, as she had already made plans.

And after that, whenever he complimented her on her skill, she brushed it off with a slight blush and an offhand comment, as though it was not at all unusual for such a young girl to jump in and feed her younger siblings as well as her bachelor uncle. Sometimes it made him wonder about his sister and how she had run her household; she must have had Maria trained to perfection.

In truth, he was exhausted from the long day, and the long days before it. Looking forward to the winter that was rapidly approaching made him feel even more at a loss. He had to face it – at times, he simply felt old. At thirty-two, hale and hearty, he certainly wasn't nearing any end to his life. He couldn't quite grasp why he felt as though everything had passed him by.

Perhaps it was the loneliness that dragged him down by the ankles. With the six-year anniversary of their moving here to Shadow Gulch on the way, it meant that it had already been six years since the children's parents had passed away from that terrible flood. He could remember all too vividly the day the telegram came. His older sister and her husband had been on their way to see an ailing friend, leaving Maria and the young twins in the care of the neighbor.

A storm had come up, and as they tried to cross a usually small and placid creek, a flash flood had come and swept them away. It had been days before their bodies were even found, and by that point, he was on his way to collect the children and take them home to stay with him. They had no other family, and there was no other choice – he was aware of the enormity of the responsibility he now had, but even so he took them in with all his heart.

Cordelia had lasted only a week…

He closed his eyes at the thought and pinched the bridge of his nose with his fingertips, feeling his head throb. Thinking of Cordelia was just as painful as remembering the loss of his sister and brother-in-law. They had only recently become engaged, of course – he'd courted Cordelia for a few months, but when she agreed to marry him, it was with obvious reluctance. And once the hollow-eyed, mourning children arrived in his home, she got one good look at the sight of her future and broke it off.

She told him she'd decided to do so long before, but he hadn't believed it. No, it was obvious the idea of caring for Maria and the twins was too much for her. It was far more than she had bargained for when she agreed to marry Verity's handsome, well-liked doctor.

He couldn't blame the children for that, of course. Nothing that had happened was their fault. And as much as it still pained him to think of Cordelia, it was more the pain of shame and anger, not of a love that had been lost. It hadn't really been lost, anyhow; it had been spitefully thrown away. At the first test of it, it had failed.

Perhaps it hadn't really been love after all.

He brought his attention back to the table in time to see that Maria was watching him with tender care and worry in her eyes. The twins, meanwhile, were chatting vivaciously about the upcoming Christmas season and what they hoped to get for presents. Their chatter made Elliot smile, even as he winced. Christmas, for him, was little more than a reminder of everything that had been lost six years ago – his sister, his bride, his youth, his energy. But for the children, this life was all they had ever known. They couldn't remember their parents, and all they knew was that their uncle Elliot had taken them in, moved them to a new little house, and bought them so many presents that first Christmas that the entire sitting room floor was inundated with shiny packages.

"Uncle Elliot," Maria said tentatively, "Hannah came for tea today, and she told me something interesting."

Elliot had to smile at the mental image of his young niece setting tea out for Hannah, who was a good three years older and quite the young lady. She lived with her brother on a ranch just outside of Shadow Gulch, only ten minutes' walk from the Sanders house at the outskirts of town. Her brother Curtis, a kind young man, had helped Elliot move their belongings in six years ago, and Hannah and Maria had become fast friends.

"Mmhmm…what's that, Maria?"

"She said her brother decided to write to a certain matrimonial agency back east, and would be married by Christmas time," she said in a rush. Elliot raised his eyebrows.

"Really? Curtis hasn't said a word to me about that. I'm surprised he would take such a step."

"Oh." Maria's eyebrows drew low as she frowned in consternation. "Is it such a bad thing to do?"

"No, not bad, exactly – dubious, I guess I'd say. You never know for sure what you're going to get with something like that."

"Oh." Maria wrung her hands and said, "Oh, dear," quietly. Her concern for her friend's brother was touching, though Elliot wasn't entirely certain why she was so very worried. He reached over and patted her hand.

"I'm sure everything will be all right. Curtis is a respectable young man, and he'll handle things right."

"Mr. Lockhart is very respectable," Maria agreed, shifting forward to look at Elliot keenly, "and I think – I think he just wanted to have a chance to find love. At least, that's what Hannah says. She says that everyone really wants to be married, and if you can't find a wife here in town, then there's no harm in looking elsewhere."

Elliot smiled. "Well, sure, I guess so."

"Do you think that's true, Uncle Elliot? Do you think that everyone really wants to be married?"

"Well," he said, thoughtfully, "I guess I'd say that marriage is what God intended for us. He made man and woman and brought them together to be husband and wife. So yes, I suppose so."

"Do you want to be married, Uncle Elliot?"

Her eyes were eager and kind. He sat back and sighed.

"Maria, it's not really a question of whether I want to be married or not. Sometimes … sometimes, things don't work out as you want them to."

She lowered her gaze to the table. "I know… I just thought, maybe…"

Somehow, he had saddened her. She must have wanted a different answer, though what answer she'd been looking for, he couldn't fathom. Maria was such a kind girl, always trying to do nice things for him and everyone around her. What did she have in mind now?

He shook his head and patted her hand again.

"Never mind," he said. "I guess I'd better listen closely to what Mattie and Martha want for Christmas. Otherwise, how will I know what not to get them?"

"Hey," cried the twins at the exact same time.

Elliot laughed and Maria broke into a smile. Yes, this was a difficult time of year, full of painful memories. But just as he had done six years ago – just as he did every year – he would put his own thoughts aside and do his best for the children that he loved as though they were his own.

# CHAPTER 2

As winter drew ever nearer, the streets of Boston were colder and more unwelcoming than they had ever been before. Bellissima Wade – Bell, to everyone who knew her – couldn't help but suspect that it was going to be a hard winter.

The first winter without her father.

Try as she might, she couldn't push the thought away. It had been only just eight months since her father had passed away from his sudden illness; she missed him terribly, and it seemed that not a day went by but that she thought of him several times. That was only natural, of course, she told herself – after all, for most of her life it had just been the two of them. A hard-working chimneysweep, he had taken care of her and seen to her every need from the time that she was very small. She, in turn, had cooked and cleaned and kept their little apartment as neat as a pin. Though her mother had passed away when she was only five years old, she had never felt a lack. Her father had been everything to her.

But everything had changed in the course of a few days, last spring.

She had gone from her happy, secure home life to being alone, plagued with mounting debts she could not afford to pay from the scant savings Henry Wade had left behind. Over the course of a few months, all the furniture and everything valuable in the little apartment had been sold in order to pay for her father's burial and to buy enough food to get by. She'd searched for a job, but employment was difficult to come by in Boston right then; there were far more people in need of work than there were positions available, and even the few factory jobs that were offered to her were such low pay she could never have afforded to live on what she made. Still, she had taken what she could get and resolved to continue searching.

But time had gone on, and her money had dwindled, and just when she was about to end up on the street, Hank Marin had finally stepped in.

She could remember the day so clearly. It had been four months since her father had passed away, and Mr. Marin had come to see her at the little apartment, bringing his wife along for the sake of propriety. Hank Marin was big on propriety – she could remember that even from her father's rueful comments on the man. He'd had the goal of going into the church, but his dream had been thwarted by his family, which demanded more immediate income. And so, he had entered the life of a chimneysweep, working alongside Henry Wade, but his sense of right and wrong – or, more accurately, of righteousness – was that of a clergyman.

"A very specific sort of right and wrong, mind you," Bell could remember her father saying with a chuckle. "He thinks very highly of his own opinions, which are right, of course. And anyone who disagrees – well, they're wrong."

Hank Marin offered, with somewhat bad grace, to take her into his home if she could not provide for herself.

"Out of respect for your departed father," he told her. "I always suspected that his soul was not as clearly on the side of the angels as one would like, but I suppose it's too late to do anything about that now. Anyhow, he is gone, and you are alone. We cannot see the daughter of an old colleague be turned out into the street – think how it would reflect on the profession."

Bell didn't think that the profession of chimneysweep would suffer much whether she had a roof over her head or not, but she knew that it would serve her best to look past the rather problematic comments which Mr. Marin had made and see the generosity of his offer. He had no real obligation to her, and the last thing her father would want was for her to be homeless.

Though she was hesitant, she agreed to come and stay with them for a time.

The time had turned into a longer period than any of them had expected. But now, near the end of November, it was almost impossible to think of simply leaving, though things in the Marin household certainly weren't as comfortable as she would have liked. Part of it was simply how Hank Marin and his wife lived – they were very stiff and formal, even with each other. And part of it was the fact that, having offered generosity, they now seemed to rather resent the fact that she had been so brash as to take them up on it.

Well, four months was a long time to live in someone else's house, she told herself, as she rounded the corner and neared the brownstone building that housed the Marin apartment. She was paying the majority of her wages toward the household expenses, of course, but she knew that it didn't cover much at all. If she could only find more work, or work that paid a little better. But she was exhausted as it was; she couldn't fathom taking on a second job.

Wrapping her coat more closely around her, she steeled herself to enter the building and face up to another uncomfortably silent evening. Dark and cold – Mr. Marin didn't approve of using too much coal in the little fireplace, nor did he approve of using enough candles to read by. It was going to be a terribly long winter; she couldn't even imagine what Christmas would be like.

She reckoned that Mr. Marin was righteous enough that he would insist that Christmas be marked only by the solemn singing of hymns at midnight.

Before she opened the door, she took a deep breath and whispered to herself, "Better the silence and a roof over your head than happiness in the cold."

She wasn't entirely sure she believed it, but it was enough to hear it spoken out loud. Besides, as she often reminded herself, at least things couldn't get any worse at the Marin household.

Unfortunately, she found out differently that evening when the silence she had so been dreading was broken by Hank Marin turning to her almost directly after the supper prayer was said and looking her over for a moment. Uncomfortably, she met his gaze, unsure of what to do. After a pause in which he seemed to assess her thoroughly, he cleared his throat.

"I have reached a decision, Miss Wade."

Even though she had lived with them for four months now, he still couldn't bring himself to call her by her first name. Well, that was all right – she didn't exactly feel so friendly with him, either.

"What is that, Mr. Marin?"

"You will get married."

Bell could feel her face go white. She blinked at him for a moment. "I – I beg your pardon?"

"That's quite all right," Mr. Marin said magnanimously. "I understand that it may come as a surprise to you, but you surely must understand that things cannot simply go on as they have. When Mrs. Marin and I opened our home to you, it was because we felt obligated to do so as Christians and chimneysweeps." He coughed politely, as though both designations were equally profound. "We did not realize quite how long you would be taking advantage of our hospitality."

Bell could hardly bring herself to speak. It was true that they had given her a place to sleep and kept her from living on the street when she was in need. But it was also true that they had begrudged every moment of their hospitality, which wasn't true generosity at all, in her opinion. But that was neither here nor there – it was the fact that he had now decided he had the right to choose what she did with her life. That was what was rendering her nearly speechless.

"I…I…I'm sure that you mean well, Mr. Marin, but…I'm not sure that I want to be married."

Mr. Marin waved a hand dismissively. "Nonsense, girl, it's the right thing to do – the God-ordained thing to do."

"But – I can't simply go out and find a husband right off the bat."

"Of course not," Mr. Marin told her. "But not to worry – I have located one for you." He continued, apparently oblivious to the fact that she was now entirely speechless, and largely with anger. "Another colleague of mine, a Mr. John Scrubbs, has recently lost his wife to a long illness and has been looking for a replacement to take care of his children. I've told him that you have no particular objection to taking care of children."

Suddenly she found her tongue.

"I don't, in fact," she said. "But I do object to being married off by someone who has no right to decide what I do with my life. I'm not going to marry Mr. John Scrubbs, Mr. Marin – or – or anyone that you decide I should. As grateful as I am for your hospitality, my father did not raise me to simply accept meekly what was imposed upon me."

"Miss Wade," said Mr. Marin severely, "meekly accepting what is imposed upon you is the role of the feminine nature."

Bell glanced swiftly at Mrs. Marin, who had her eyes on her plate. She felt a stab of sympathy for the woman.

"Perhaps for some," she said, "but not for all. I'm sorry, Mr. Marin, but I simply won't agree. And as you are not my guardian, you have no right to speak for me."

Hank Marin leaned back in his chair and regarded her. "In that case, if you will not accept the headship of living under my household – I will ask you to leave."

Shocked, she stared at him. "Leave?"

"Yes. I will not demand that you leave tonight, but I expect you to be gone tomorrow morning by breakfast time."

Bell felt tears start in her eyes – not at the prospect of leaving the Marin household, but simply at how quickly things could change. She had lost her father after an illness of only a few days. She had lost her home within four months. Now she was about to be turned out on the street, and there was nothing she could do about it.

At least she still had some dignity and pride left – though it warred with her pragmaticism in the moment. After a brief skirmish, the pragmaticism won out.

She nodded and stood up from the table.

"I will," she said. "Thank you, Mr. Marin, Mrs. Marin – thank you for your hospitality."

She left the room before he could say anything – and before she could say anything else.

The night was long, and sleep was elusive, which came as no surprise. As the morning sun struggled up and out from behind the clouds, she packed her few possessions and left the apartment for the last time. She would not miss it, she knew, but she had to find somewhere to go.

The idea of being married and cared for was certainly not a bad one. It was simply the fact that he had spoken for her, had arranged things without asking her, she took offense to. If she'd had any prospects for marriage – things might be different, but she had none. She was twenty-one years old and knew in an off-hand way that most men thought her very pretty. But she wasn't about to go out and just marry the first person on the street simply to have a roof over her head.

Wondering what would become of her and missing her father terribly, she took to the streets of Boston, walking quickly to try and keep warm.

Shortly after eight o'clock, she saw a line of girls ahead of her. At first, she thought that it might be a soup kitchen, and pressed forward eagerly, hoping that she might preserve a bit more of her small savings. But as she drew closer, curiously looking around the group, she saw the sign on the building ahead.

*McKeegan's Matrimonial Agency*

She came to a standstill, pondering over it, and the girl behind her nearly ran into her.

"Hey, watch out there."

"Oh, goodness, I'm sorry," Bell said, putting a hand out to steady the girl, who shook her head with a rueful smile.

"That's all right. It's probably my own fault for not looking where I was going. But I was trying to get in line before it gets too much longer. Are you coming along, too?"

"I don't even know what the line is for."

"Oh." The girl waved a hand airily. "It's to be matched with bachelors and become a Mail Order Bride." She got a good look at Bell's expression and laughed. "It's not as funny as it sounds. The matrimonial agency is very good about making sure the men are respectable."

"If they're so respectable, why are they needing to find brides from an agency?" Bell couldn't help but ask.

The girl shrugged. "Most of them are from the territories, or even all the way out west, like California. You know, the wild country. It's hard to find a wife out there, I bet."

"I suppose that makes sense."

"Anyhow, they write to the agency and tell 'em what they're looking for, and the agency matches them up with a girl here and sends them on their way. They send a fee, and the agency pays for the ticket. Say, you're not married, are you?"

Bell shook her head, feeling a blush start on her cheeks. She had never thought much about the fact that she was still unmarried at her age, but after the discussion with Mr.

Marin the night before and her own thoughts this morning, this question seemed rather pointed.

"Do you have a job?"

"I do – but not a very good one."

"Well," said the girl, and shrugged. "Might as well see what they've got for you. What's stopping you?"

Bell opened her mouth to answer – and then closed it again abruptly. What was stopping her, indeed? She had no family, no close friends. Her job wasn't enough to sustain her, and now she had no place to live. She objected to Mr. Marin finding a husband for her, but this would be different. This would be her own choice.

On impulse, she asked, "I don't suppose they ever find a match for you on the very first visit?"

The girl shrugged again. "I hope so, myself. Why? Are you that anxious to start anew?"

Bell took a deep breath.

"As a matter of fact," she said, "I am."

# CHAPTER 3

The west-bound train was crowded and full, and Bell edged her way onto it, feeling her heartbeat so strongly she could feel it thrum in her lips.

This was it – she had made the decision, and she was on her way. There was no going back now.

She didn't want to go back.

Even so, as she made her way to a seat near the center of the train car, she couldn't help but fight against the rush of emotions that swept over her. After all, Boston had been her home her entire life. She left her father there, buried in the cemetery, to be blanketed in snow as the winter came onward. And she wouldn't be there to bring flowers to his grave in the spring.

She turned her face to the window and dashed at the tears that came to her eyes.

"Are you all right?"

The voice was kind, but the kindness itself made it even more difficult to keep from breaking down into tears. Biting her lip, Bell turned to see who it was. The speaker was a young woman, not much more than a year or two older than Bell herself. She was the complete opposite of Bell, with wavy blonde hair while Bell's was straight and dark, and a rosy-cheeked complexion while Bell was darker. The concerned smile on her pretty face made Bell take to her immediately.

"Yes," she managed, with another preventative swipe at her eyes. "I'm just – well, I'm leaving Boston behind, and it's the only home I've ever known."

"Are you alone?"

Bell nodded.

"Good," said the young woman promptly, and sat down right next to her. "I mean to say, it isn't good that you're alone – though I am, too, if that helps at all. But I'm glad this seat was empty. To be honest, I was beginning to fear that I would have to ride all the way to Idaho standing up in the aisle."

Despite her strong emotions, Bell couldn't help but chuckle at the young woman's frank comment.

"Surely some gallant young man would have given up his seat for you."

"I don't know about that. I'm leaving Boston myself because there's a shortage of gallant young men."

Something occurred to Bell. "Did you say that you are going to Idaho?"

"Indeed."

"That's where I'm headed, too."

"Really." The girl leaned back and looked her over. "Don't tell me that you're going to be a Mail Order Bride."

"Yes." Bell told her excitedly. "You as well?"

"Yes."

The two grinned at each other.

"All that's left," said the girl, "is for us to discover that we are heading to the same exact town – but that's beyond belief, don't you think?"

Bell shook her head. "Most certainly."

"We shouldn't even tell each other where we're going. Because it won't be the same town, at all."

"As far away as you can get and still be in Idaho."

"And if it is, it would be a…" She was clearly searching for the right way to describe the enormity of the coincidence.

"A Christmas miracle," Bell finished for her.

"Yes," the girl laughed, "that's it exactly. Well, all right, then. We'll both say the name of the town, on the count of three. Ready?"

"Shadow Gulch." they said simultaneously, without even waiting for the count, and burst into harmonious laughter. The girl stuck her hand out for Bell to shake, smiling widely.

"Lorna Olsen," she said.

Bell shook her hand. "Bell Wade. I can't believe it."

"Me neither." Lorna squeezed her hand. "I'm going to meet a man named Mr. Lockhart." She fumbled in her pocketbook and retrieved a folded piece of paper, which she smoothed out and waved at Bell. "Let's see – yes – Curtis Lockhart. He is twenty-five years old and works on a ranch outside of the town of Shadow Gulch." She turned an avid gaze on Bell. "Who have you been matched with?"

Bell could remember the details of her match by heart. She had gone over and over them in her mind in the past eight hours, and they seemed to be ingrained.

"A doctor," she said, "by name of Elliot Sanders. He's thirty-two and is the guardian of his two nieces and one nephew. He only wrote his letter to the agency just this past week; evidently it was a sudden decision, for he didn't even ask to correspond with the match or the agency. He simply asked for someone to be sent."

"I reckon he needs help with those children," said Lorna, nodding. Bell nodded back.

"I suppose so," she said. "Well, that's all right. I don't mind."

"And you could arrange your affairs to leave this quickly? If the letter only came this week…"

"If you want to call it 'arranging my affairs,' I suppose… yes. In fact, I only applied with the agency just this morning, and I asked for any match they had that could be made quickly."

"Goodness." Lorna shook her head in admiration. "How brave you are. I've been corresponding with my fellow for weeks now, trying to get my nerve up to make the journey."

Bell laughed.

"I guess I haven't known you long, but I certainly wouldn't think that you lacked nerves."

"You're right there," Lorna admitted, smiling. "Well, just think of it, Bell Wade – both of us on the same train heading to the same town. We thought we were alone, and we weren't, all along. I believe we are meant to be friends."

Bell smiled at her. Her tears were entirely forgotten by now.

"I think so too," she said.

"And just think – we'll both be married by Christmas."

Bell caught her breath at the thought. Again, her whole life seemed to be changing from one instant to the next.

"Yes," she said. "Like you and me meeting like this – a Christmas miracle."

# CHAPTER 4

On December the first, Elliot had a feeling that his prediction about the difficult winter was already coming true. The front room at the little doctor's office was packed with patients, including the entirety of the Philips family.

He waved them back into the examination room, and they came as a group: Eddie Philips and his young wife Mariah, and their three little ones, all under five years old.

"Well, Eddie, what seems to be the trouble?"

The other man sniffled and smiled at the same time.

"I reckon it's just a cold, Doc, but Mariah was worried with the little ones, so we thought we'd come and make sure."

"Aha." He lifted James, the older boy, up onto the examination table and palpated behind his ears. "Am I right in thinking that all of you have taken sick?"

"Yes, Doc, that's right. Me and Mariah, not so much, but James and little Bitsy are feeling it more. Peter's just got the sniffles, like me."

Elliot carried out his standard examination on James and Peter, ending with Bitsy, who was just about to turn two and didn't appreciate this stranger pressing behind her ears. She shrieked, and Mariah stepped forward to take her into her arms the moment that Elliot was done. Elliot washed his hands at the basin, watching the young parents with their children. Eddie and Mariah were excellent examples of parenthood, he reflected; they were patient with their three little ones, but not indulgent. Stern, but not strict.

Mariah whispered comfort to her baby girl, and Eddie put James back up on the table next to Peter and handed them each a handkerchief to blow their noses.

Even in sickness, they were the perfect little family – and Elliot felt the sight suddenly twist at his heart.

That was what it should have been like for himself and Cordelia. Raising Maria, Mattie, and Martha – and raising their own children, too. They should have been a perfect little family, right from the beginning, six years ago…

Biting his lip, he turned back to the basin for a moment until he could gather his self-control. There was nothing he could do about the past, he reminded himself. He could only do his best with the future.

Still, the mental image of the family he should have had, and never did, stuck with him for the rest of the day, souring how he felt. Even as the Christmas holiday stepped ever nearer, filling the people around him with the jovial spirit of winter, he felt himself sinking further and further into his own mind, wrapping his emotions in layers of cloth as though preparing to tuck them away for the long winter.

He was in quite the despondent mood by the time he arrived home that evening. It was just a little bit earlier than he usually got home, thanks to several quick diagnoses amongst the sick in his waiting room – most of them ailed only from the common cold, he was glad to find – and he caught his little family unawares. Slipping into the front door, he hung up his coat and hat and followed the sound of Maria's voice as it drifted down the hallway.

She was reading Dickens to them – Pickwick Papers, he could recognize it from the way she was speaking – and he had to pause and listen, smiling to himself. He loved to hear her read. She had always opined that it was just as important for the twins to hear the words read aloud as it was for them to read themselves. Though he would have expected something a bit more in the spirit of the season, based on the twins' excitement – but perhaps that was why she had opted for Pickwick Papers rather than A Christmas Carol, for example. Perhaps she was trying to calm down the excitement a little...the twins were certainly notorious for getting over-excited, leading inevitably to a crash of some sort, usually a fight between the two of them.

He stepped around the corner, keeping as quiet as possible, and glanced in on them through the open door to the sitting room. Maria had kept the fire that he started this morning going through the day; it was certainly cold enough to warrant it. The little sitting room was cozy and warm, the firelight flickering, the oil lamp on the table beside the sofa burning away cheerfully. Maria sat in the middle of the sofa, with Mattie on one side and Martha on the other.

Mattie had been named after his father, Matthew; Martha had been named after Elliot's mother, who had passed away long before the twins were born. Maria herself was properly Eleanor Maria, named for her mother Eleanor and great-aunt Maria – Aunt Maria had passed away when Elliot was twenty, and, of course, poor Eleanor had died when the twins were only just over a year. Sometimes it struck Elliot deeply to think of how all three of these children were named for people who were long gone.

Sometimes it made his heart ache to think of how much these children had lost.

He wanted to gather them up and take care of them as best he could, though he knew that he was so limited in his capacity. To think of that made him ever more resentful of Cordelia – no, not resentful, exactly. He simply didn't understand it. How could she, how could anyone, turn her back on these innocent and trusting souls, who wanted only to be loved?

How could he begin to regret the way that things had happened, or wish that things were different now?

He stepped forward, and the three children were at last alerted to his presence. The warmth of the greeting which he received was reward enough for the long and stressful day he'd had, and he picked up the twins, one in each arm, and smiled at Maria. Yes, it was true that this was not the life he'd expected to end up with. But since there was little hope of it changing –he was determined to be grateful for what he had.

# CHAPTER 5

The beginning of December was sliding haphazardly into the middle when the train at last puffed into the small town of Shadow Gulch, Idaho. It had been quite the adventure. As things went along, the passengers were sloughed off little by little, most of them disembarking well before the western territories were reached. But Lorna stuck by Bell's side faithfully, and the two girls were such close friends by the end of the trip that it seemed impossible that they'd only just met a short ten days before.

That was what happened with trying circumstances, Bell reflected. When you found a friendly face, you clung on all the more tightly.

"Can you believe that we're here at last?" Lorna asked eagerly, so close to the window that her nose was practically flattened on the glass.

"It seems almost impossible."

"But here we are. Oh, what a precious little town. No wonder people live in places like this – it's so quaint, especially compared to Boston. Look, all the buildings are lined with wood. I don't see a single brick wall."

Lorna's excitement was contagious, though Bell's stomach was churning with nerves. She felt caught somewhere between the thrill of finally beginning her new life, of having escaped the depressing circumstances of her life in Boston – and apprehension about the future. It hadn't occurred to her until now, but suppose she – well, suppose she just didn't like this Doctor Sanders?

Well, she told herself sternly, there wasn't anything she could do about it now. And at the very least, it was a decision she had made for herself – not one Hank Marin had made for her.

As they made ready to step onto the platform, Lorna reached over and took her hand, holding tightly.

They went down the steps together and found themselves in a whole different world.

Lorna was right, Shadow Gulch was certainly quaint – and small – and everything was built with wooden boards. It was cleaner than Bell might have expected, too, though she supposed that the summer would bring gusts of dust from these dirt streets that might tinge everything a dirty brown. Now, though, they had evidently already had enough rain to tamp the streets down tightly, though there wasn't much mud to be seen. Yet, anyhow – with these dirt streets, without a cobble to be seen, there seemed little doubt that they would be a welter of mud as soon as the rain really got going.

If there was much rain in this part of the world…Bell wasn't sure. It suddenly hit her with a great deal of force, that she was somewhere entirely new with no experience or expectations whatsoever. She clutched even more tightly at Lorna's hand.

Her new friend squeezed back and led her forward.

"Come on, let's go find our husbands."

There were not many people waiting for the train, which Bell supposed wasn't all that surprising – after all, it was a small town. Like her friend, she craned her neck to look back and forth, searching for anyone who might reasonably be the man she was planning to marry.

"Let's make a pact," Lorna said quickly. "No matter what happens, we'll be friends here in Shadow Gulch. Oh, I hope that our homes are not too far away from each other."

"Of course, we'll be friends," Bell said. "I can't imagine the miracle bringing us together and then letting us fall apart."

She caught another swift smile from her friend before Lorna returned to the search. In reward for her eagerness, a young man detached himself from the other waiting strangers and came forward. He had his hands shoved in his pockets and a bashful air. A young woman followed him, with an eager smile, and a girl of about fifteen came along with her.

"Goodness," Bell commented, "it appears that you're being welcomed by a committee."

"Oh, my."

The tow-headed young man, as blonde as Lorna herself, grinned sheepishly as he approached.

"I don't suppose you'd be Miss Lorna Olsen, would you?"

Lorna was already blushing, though her forthright manner did not fail her. "I am indeed. And you must be Mr. Curtis Lockhart."

The young man nodded, and Lorna burst out, "Gosh, I'm glad to finally meet you. It seems as though we've already known each other for ages, and yet here we are, only just now meeting in person."

He stuck his hand out, and she seized it and pumped it enthusiastically.

Shrinking slightly to one side, Bell couldn't help but continue to look around for the sign of her own waiting match. With Lorna's intended groom here before them, she hoped devoutly that her husband was at least half as handsome and friendly as Curtis Lockhart – but the important thing, of course, was that he be present.

To her surprise, however, the younger girl stepped forward. She had a shy smile, thick brown hair in two plaits, and wide blue eyes.

"Excuse me, miss – are you Bellissima Wade?"

Bell smiled at her in response. It was impossible not to smile at that sweet, open face. "Why, yes, dear, I am."

"Oh, good." The young girl clasped her hands together, her eyes shining. "I was half afraid that you wouldn't come after all, not without talking to my uncle first – but, well, here you are." She beamed at Bell, seeming almost at a loss for words. Lorna, slightly distracted from her own bliss at finally meeting Mr. Lockhart, exchanged curious glances with Bell.

"Your uncle? Who is your uncle?"

"My uncle," said the girl clearly, "is Doctor Elliot Sanders."

Bell's smile grew even wider.

"Why, I see." she exclaimed. "I should have thought of it. Of course, as a doctor, he must be incredibly busy today, and has sent his niece to meet me."

"How thoughtful," Lorna said.

"Well, er…not exactly," said the niece of Doctor Elliot Sanders. She exchanged a glance with the other young woman, who took it upon herself to explain.

"What Maria means to say is that Doctor Sanders is, of course, very busy – he's the only doctor in Shadow Gulch, after all. But there are other explanations needed, and she will provide them very soon. In the meantime, she's asked me to put you up, Miss Wade."

Curtis Lockhart looked over at her sharply. "She did?"

Bell blinked blankly at her. "I'm sorry, I'm not sure who you are…"

"She's my sister," said Curtis. "Hannah Lockhart. My younger sister, who apparently forgot to mention anything to me about any Miss Wade staying with us…"

"Oh, but that would be delightful," Lorna broke in. She clutched Bell's arm. "We've become very good friends on the train, and since neither of us know anyone else here in Shadow Gulch, it would be so reassuring to have each other even if just for a while."

It was clear by the slightly concerned expression on Curtis Lockhart's face that he wasn't entirely happy with the thought of sharing his newly arrived bride-to-be. Bell, meanwhile, was still desperately trying to fathom the reason why Doctor Sanders might not have come to meet her, if it wasn't simply that he was too busy. The confusion, the questions, and the sudden overwhelming feeling of being in a strange place surrounded by strangers was all too much for her. She pressed her hands to her cheeks.

"This is all so confusing…" she murmured.

To her surprise, it was Maria, the little niece of the man she was intending to marry, who comforted her with a hand on her arm and a warm smile.

"All will be clear in time," she said. "Everything is going to be all right, Miss Wade."

Despite her distress, Bell had to smile at the young woman and her warmth, which seemed to belong to a much older and more experienced adult.

"Thank you, dear," she said. "I'm sure it will. And please, you must call me Bell. Everyone does."

Maria nodded.

"My name is Maria Darling," she said, "and I'm sorry for all the confusion. I've left the children for far too long, and I'd better be getting supper on the table too. But don't worry – I'll come to visit the ranch tomorrow, if I may." This appeal was diplomatically made to Curtis Lockhart, who seemed to be soothed by her deference, and gave a genial smile and a nod. "Good, then. Have a nice evening, everyone. I'll see you tomorrow morning."

Then the girl slipped away, leaving the rest watching after her, with a kind of admiration written on each face. Lorna shook her head.

"I don't know much about Shadow Gulch, Idaho," she said, "but if that girl is running for mayor, I'd campaign for her."

Hannah Lockhart laughed.

"She has a way about her, doesn't she?" she said. "She's always been older and wiser than her years. Wiser than most people far older than her, in fact," she said teasingly, nudging her brother in the ribs. Curtis grinned and nudged her back.

"Well," he said, "if Hannah isn't going to fill us in on what's going on, I guess we'd better just go have supper and pretend to be content to wait."

Lorna smiled at him. It was the smile of an infatuated woman.

"I don't think I'll have to pretend," she said.

As the little group left the station, Bell trailed along, wondering to herself what she'd gotten herself into – and what the future might possibly hold.

# CHAPTER 6

The next day seemed to take forever in coming. The evening passed swiftly enough, with supper and light banter between brother and sister and brother and bride-to-be – Bell herself kept quiet, feeling rather out of place despite the efforts of the others to make her feel included. She was grateful to be with her friend, and the Lockharts were perfectly friendly, as well, but until she understood the circumstances and what her future would be, she couldn't be entirely at ease.

Curtis Lockhart ran the ranch on behalf of its owner, Douglas Gall, who lived in Lewiston and owned multiple ranches across the territories. He seemed young to have such authority, but his conversation and serious mien showed that he was quite dedicated to his job, and the neatness and efficiency of the ranch proved the wisdom of Mr. Gall in establishing this young man as he had done.

It was also clear from the very beginning that Lorna had made the right decision in coming to Shadow Gulch to marry him; at least, from the standpoint of her happiness, it was very clear. All through supper, and again the next morning as they gathered for breakfast early before Curtis headed out to attend to running the ranch, Lorna stared avidly at him. She seemed delighted with each new aspect she discovered, and any vaguely humorous comment that he made was sure to be rewarded with peals of laughter.

In fact, she evidently regarded her husband-to-be as the pinnacle of manly perfection, and Bell was desperately trying to hide the fact that it was rather – well – annoying.

She knew, though, that she wouldn't feel that way if her own circumstances were the same. Indeed, she would likely encourage Lorna to ever taller heights of enthusiasm and bliss, simply because she felt the same way and could sympathize. As things were, however, she felt as though she was missing out, as though Lorna simply had something she did not – and until Maria Darling came to explain herself, this was, for all intents and purposes, true.

This certainly wasn't what she had been expecting when she made the sudden decision to leave Boston behind and travel to Shadow Gulch.

But now she was here, she reminded herself, and the only thing she could do was wait – as patiently as possible.

In the meantime, she tried to focus on how happy she was for her friend. Lorna had what every girl deserved – love at first sight. She'd been corresponding with Curtis for a few months, and it had given her a valuable insight into his character. From the moment she stepped off the train, she was ready to fall in love with the man she was going to marry, and now that they were together, her happiness was complete.

Bell was not a negative person by nature and reflecting on her friend's joy was the main reason she was able to get through the evening and the morning after as well as she did.

Besides, she would remind herself now and then, if she hadn't made the choice to leave Boston and come here, she might very well be married off to Hank Marin's chimneysweep colleague and taking care of his children by now.

Taking care of children wasn't the main problem, of course – now that she had met Maria, she was even more curious as to the nature of the other niece and nephew for whom Elliot Sanders was guardian. If Maria was anything to go by, they would be a delight, not to mention rather unusual.

At last, with breakfast over and done with and Curtis off to see to his morning chores, there came a knock on the kitchen door, and Maria slipped through with a tentative smile.

"Come in, come in," Hannah told her, ushering her into the warm kitchen and giving her a gentle shove in the direction of the fireplace. "It's freezing outside, you must be so cold. Where are the twins?"

"I left them with Mrs. Hardy for a little while. She put them right to work helping her to bake Christmas cookies, so they're happy as can be and won't miss me while I'm gone." She rubbed her hands and held them out to the fire, giving Lorna and Bell a smile over her shoulder. "Hello, Miss Olsen – hello, Bell."

"Please, call me Lorna. Hello, dear."

"Good morning, Maria," Bell said. Lorna nudged her.

"Look who is deciding to pretend as though she hasn't avidly been waiting for Maria to show up all morning long. Every five seconds she was looking at the door or the window."

"I wasn't," Bell said, fighting a blush. "Perhaps I was – a bit concerned that something might happen to delay her. But that is all."

"Goodness," said Lorna, rolling her eyes comically. "Let's not beat around the bush. Maria, we've all been dying to hear the truth of matters, and Hannah here hasn't given us a peep."

"She doesn't know, really," Maria said, coming to join them at the table. "I haven't told anyone – though she may suspect."

Hannah shrugged one shoulder.

"Suspicion isn't the truth," she said. "All I know is that, whatever you've done, it has been for the best of reasons."

"Come on, then," Lorna urged the younger girl. "Fill us in."

Maria took a deep breath before she began.

"The truth is, it's all about my uncle Elliot," she said. "He's a good man – the best – isn't he?" She addressed this to Hannah, who nodded at once. "My parents passed away six years ago, and he took us in without hesitation. I've never heard him so much as daydream about what his life might have been like without us, even though it cost him dearly. You see, at the time my parents died, Uncle Elliot lived in Verity, Idaho, and was engaged to be married to a girl named Cordelia." She cast her eyes to the table, shaking her head. "He was very much in love with her, but she was not deserving of it in the least. When she realized he had taken on my younger siblings and me and would serve as our guardian until we grew up, she broke off their engagement and left him at once."

Bell could picture it all too clearly, and her heart went out to him.

"He must have been distraught," she said. "To have lost family, and then to lose the woman he loved simply because he was doing the right thing."

"I don't believe she thought it was the right thing," said Maria slowly. "Uncle Elliot doesn't know this, but when she told him she was leaving, I could hear every word they said. They were just inside the kitchen, and I was sitting with the twins in the next room over. She asked him to give us up, to turn us over to an orphanage, and said that if he did that, she would stay with him."

She sighed quietly. "But he refused at once, and never so much as gave it a moment's thought. She told him she wasn't ready to be a mother to three children and could not help him to raise us. He told her he would do everything that must be done and asked only that she give us her love and attention. And she…"

The young girl gritted her teeth. "She laughed in his face. It was so mean, so cruel – she told him she wasn't even sure she could give him her love and attention and wasn't about to promise it to three brats she didn't even know. I believe he was about to ask her to leave, then, but she didn't wait for it. She left, and she didn't ever come back."

Bell, her heart full of sadness and sympathy, reached out and pressed the girl's hand. It was the first time she had seen the young woman look her own age. Maria accepted her wordless comfort with grace and appreciation and continued on.

"A few weeks after that, Uncle Elliot packed us up and moved us here, to Shadow Gulch. We got settled into the house just a few days before Christmas." She glanced over at Hannah, who nodded and smiled encouragingly. "Hannah and Curtis came and helped us, and a few of the other neighbors too. The town was grateful to have a new doctor. They weren't able to give Uncle Elliot any more pay, and I know that it's been hard on him to raise the three of us with not much money coming in. I remember that first Christmas, though, he somehow managed to fill the whole sitting room with presents…"

She sank into the memory for a moment, eyes far away and a sad smile on the corners of her mouth. "He didn't know what to do for three children who had lost their parents, so he did everything he could think of. He didn't know how to be a father, and barely knew how to be an uncle, but he's thrown everything into it. And he deserves something better than the memory of Cordelia. He deserves something good, a love of his own that will love him back." Again, she glanced at Hannah, who in turn glanced at Lorna.

"I guess it's really my fault that all this is happening," Hannah said. "I'm the one who told Maria about writing for a Mail Order Bride. Of course, Curtis made his own decision to do so – and I didn't know that Maria would take it upon herself. But dear Maria, how did you gather the money to pay for Bell's train ticket?"

"I… I had it saved from when my parents died… Uncle Elliot wouldn't take it when we came to him. He refused, saying it was our money from our parents. I… I used it all."

"What?" Bell cried, both alarmed and touched. "Oh, dear. You shouldn't have. That was yours—"

Maria looked downcast at the gentle reproach. "I only wanted Uncle Elliot to be happy," she said. "And Hannah said Curtis was just over the moon – that's what I want for Uncle. He works too much. Everyone likes him, but he doesn't have any close friends because he's always either working or with the twins and me. He must want a family, just as everyone else does."

Bell still couldn't quite put words to the rush of emotions she was feeling. She turned a helpless glance on Lorna, who rallied and stepped into the quiet.

"Perhaps he does," she said, "but he may not be entirely happy when he finds that his niece has made such a big decision for him."

"Oh, dear," said Maria, wringing her hands. "I-I didn't think about that."

"Furthermore, the agreement to become a Mail Order Bride is a very serious one," Lorna continued. "Bell traveled all the way out here on the understanding that she would be provided for, with a husband and a roof over her head. But if the other party doesn't even know about it, how can he be expected to hold to that agreement?"

"I know," Maria said, her head sinking ever lower. "I s'pose it was a very silly thing to do."

Bell couldn't take it anymore. Maria was a sweet, humble, heartfelt girl, and it was obvious that everything she'd done had been from good motives and the love in her heart for her uncle. She reached out and put a hand on the girl's shoulder. Maria looked up and met her eyes.

"I don't know your uncle," Bell said, "and I don't know that he will want to marry me – or anyone, for that matter. But the story you tell of him, the way you talk about him, makes me believe he is truly a good man. And he will understand once you explain it to him. After that – well, you must leave it up to him to make the choice." She paused, thinking of her own painful experience. "Believe me, Maria, it's no small thing to try to make decisions for others. Especially when it comes to whom they should marry."

Maria's eyes were beginning to light up from within, and Bell recognized the surging fire of hope, slowly being rekindled.

"You mean that you'll try to be his Mail Order Bride, if he wants you to?"

Bell smiled at her. "I'll certainly give it my best."

"Oh."

The girl was up, around the table, and wrapping her arms around Bell in an instant. Bell laughed, embracing Maria in return.

Next to her, Lorna observed with a smile, "Well, we thought we'd both be married by Christmas. I suppose there's still a chance."

Bell hugged Maria tighter.

"Yes," she said. "There's always a chance."

# CHAPTER 7

Influenza, la grippe, a broken ankle, general stomach complaints, and several cases of the common cold had come and gone through that day by the time that Elliot saw his last patient. Closing the door behind Mr. Adams, Elliot took a moment to stretch out his back, swinging his arms behind him and feeling joints pop and crackle. He turned and looked at the waiting room, which was empty at last, and sighed.

Would he ever get used to working in a town like this? At least in Verity, he'd worked as part of a practice with another doctor. Doctor Moore had been older, wiser, more pragmatic. It had been a relief to have him around…

But he couldn't start regretting things he'd left behind in Verity. Not now.

He shook the thought away from him and fetched his hat and coat from the inner room before he banked down the fire and left for the night.

He had finally learned the art of admitting to himself he was exhausted. He still had difficulty in admitting it to anyone else, but at least once he could face up to facts, he could take steps to fix the issue. In this case, the steps seemed to be going home and to bed at once. He would have to tell Maria he was simply not feeling hungry that evening, and ask her to wake him at his usual time if he did not appear…

The short walk home had never seemed so long, and by the time his dragging footsteps led him up to the front door of his little house, he was yawning profusely. To his consternation, however, he heard voices as soon as he set foot inside – some voices he recognized, and others he did not.

They weren't in the kitchen, either. They were in the dining room, which meant company.

The Sanders household hardly ever saw real company. The most they had was generally the neighbor lady, Mrs. Hardy, who gave Martha sewing lessons, and Curtis and Hannah Lockhart, who were too familiar and comfortable to be relegated to the more formal dining room, even when they came over for supper, which was rare. However, as Elliot listened from just down the hall, he was relieved to find that he did recognize Curtis' reedy voice. It was the voices he did not recognize, however, that were the sources of worry.

He took a moment and steeled himself before entering the dining room.

Maria caught sight of him first.

"Uncle Elliot."

Martha and Mattie, who were seated neatly at the table, squirmed out of their chairs and rushed him, as they had the habit of doing. Elliot picked them up, one in each arm, and observed the array of faces that was seated at his dining table.

There was Curtis – praise the Lord, Elliot thought irreverently – and his sister Hannah. Alongside the two familiar faces were two faces that were unfamiliar. Both young women, somewhere around Hannah's age, perhaps, or a little older. One with a round face and curly blonde hair. The other thinner, narrower, with a striking sort of dark beauty that sent a thumping through his heart. He caught her eyes almost immediately, and looked away just as quickly, unsure of what the feeling was that was surging in his chest. He knew only that he felt rather self-conscious and delicate about the fact that Martha and Mattie were attempting to squish his face into a more genial expression.

Maria came over to him, taking Mattie from him and tucking him expertly onto her hip.

"I hope you don't mind, Uncle Elliot, but I've invited the Lockharts to join us for supper tonight – and their guests, of course."

"So I see," Elliot said, reaching out to pinch her cheek quickly. "I suppose I don't mind – though it's been a terribly long day, Maria."

Her smile was sympathetic. "I know, Uncle. I'd hoped that it would be less busy, and you could come home earlier, and then I would have asked you about it. But I ran over to see Hannah this morning, and when I met Lorna and Bell, it seemed only natural to invite them over for supper. After all, you're the one who has trained us to be hospitable."

Elliot didn't think this was true at all – if anything, his niece had trained him to be at least somewhat more hospitable – but it didn't seem like the kind of thing to argue about in front of guests. He returned his attention to the smiling, waiting faces around the table and managed a smile of his own, advancing and setting Martha back in her seat.

"Ahem – um – good evening, all. Curtis. Miss Hannah." He nodded to them, and they nodded back. Curtis was grinning with an expression Elliot hadn't ever seen on him, some combination of happiness and pride. "Won't you introduce me to your friends?"

"I sure will, Doc," Curtis said. He turned to the pretty blonde girl, who sat next to him, and said, "This here is Lorna Olsen, Miss Lorna Olsen – soon to be Mrs. Curtis Lockhart. As a matter of fact, I proposed this afternoon, and we're to be married three days before Christmas."

Lorna turned to meet his gaze, blushing, and suddenly Elliot understood why Curtis looked the way he did. Of course, he had spoken some time ago about his desire to get married and how he was contemplating writing for a bride from back east – come to think of it, Maria herself had mentioned it, hadn't she? He had been so busy he could hardly remember and had scarcely taken much note of it when she'd brought it up. But now, faced with the reality, it suddenly made sense.

He had thought at the time it was something of a foolish idea, to write to a complete stranger. How could you expect she would be true, when you didn't even know her? Of course, his inner self argued, there was no knowing for certain a girl would be true even when you did know her… but that was an argument that should be saved for a later time, when he wasn't watching this evidence of his young friend discovering love for the first time. Had he turned into a skeptic? Was he become a bitter person?

Yes, that was a brief stab of jealousy in his heart, brought on by seeing Curtis' obvious happiness. But he could overcome that, if he chose. He would simply focus on being happy for his friend, instead.

He cleared his throat, and Lorna Olsen glanced back at him, still blushing.

"I'm sorry," she said, "I do find Curtis to be a little… distracting. I'm pleased to meet you, Doctor Sanders."

"Likewise, I'm sure."

But not as pleased as Curtis was, he thought, but did not say that out loud. Instead, he took his seat at the head of the table. The other stranger, the unknown woman with the dark hair and arresting eyes, was seated immediately to his right. She gave him a quick, demure smile and then dropped her eyes back down to the table.

Maria sat next to him on his left.

"And this is Bell Wade," she said, once it became obvious that Lorna wasn't going to introduce her friend. "She is also from Boston and traveled out with Lorna."

"I see," said Elliot. It struck him as a little odd that another girl should come along with Lorna Olsen, when she had agreed to come as a Mail Order Bride, but he supposed he didn't really know enough about the process to pass any judgement. Besides, she was very pretty, and he wasn't about to object to her presence at his supper table.

Maria and Hannah brought the food to the table in great steaming pots and platters, and the chatter quickly died down once everyone was confronted with the prospect of actually eating. Elliot was aware they must have been waiting for him to return home from the office, and he staved off a feeling of guilt at having held them up. After all, he hadn't known they were coming.

Still, the least he could do was avoid making them wait any longer.

He smiled at the group around the table, fighting once again with his own exhaustion.

"Let us say grace," he said, and bowed his head.

He said thanks as swiftly as possible – as swiftly as he could without making it seem rushed and ungrateful – and then lifted his head again. Maria began to portion out the meal, and he took a moment to look around him as the group settled back into friendly, comfortable chatter. Curtis and Lorna were deeply engrossed in each other. Hannah was teasing Mattie. Martha was helpfully passing out the plates as Maria filled them. And the unknown factor, this young lady named Bell Wade, seemed very intent on avoiding his gaze, though he kept catching himself looking in her direction.

She was very pretty…

Again, he wondered at what, precisely, had brought her here to Shadow Gulch, all the way from Boston. Perhaps she was a Mail Order Bride, like her friend Lorna, and something had gone wrong.

Or perhaps she was just looking to start anew.

Regardless of the circumstances, he reminded himself sharply, it didn't matter in the least. She was a friend of a friend, and nothing more. This odd feeling in his chest was symptomatic of his extreme exhaustion, that was all. It wasn't because he found himself so intrigued by her that he couldn't even think straight.

No, no, no. That wasn't it at all.

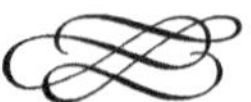

# CHAPTER 8

The day set for Lorna's wedding to Curtis Lockhart was rapidly approaching, along with the festivities more traditionally associated with the Christmas season. Because both the wedding and Christmas were so close together, it was impossible to avoid linking one with the other. It seemed that half the time was spent making Christmas stockings and fruitcake, and the other was spent sewing lace onto Lorna's wedding dress and listening to her giggle about how handsome Curtis was.

The longer she spent with Lorna, the more Bell liked her. She was funny and forthright and frank, but she had a heart of gold. Still, the longer she heard her talk about Curtis Lockhart, the more Bell wished their wedding would hurry up and get over with. She was growing fairly sick to the teeth of hearing her infatuated friend enumerate the many joys and perfections of her groom, and she rather hoped that actual married life would put some of those qualities in perspective.

Especially was she a bit more tired of it now that she had someone else which whom to compare Curtis Lockhart.

She couldn't imagine that any man would ever look like a better prospect when standing alongside someone like Doctor Elliot Sanders.

She had to admit it – she had been taken with him right from the very first moment she had seen him. No, even before that – as she had listened to Maria recount the story of how her Uncle Elliot had chosen to defend his nieces and nephew and even faced up to losing his fiancée, rather than turn out three innocent children who had just lost their parents - she had felt her heart slowly grow and contract inside her, as though her heart itself was breathing deeply. Bell had always been drawn to stories of heroics, and she knew that sometimes the most important sort of heroics were the kind that went unsung. The small ones, the little acts of heroism that made the world a better place.

She had a feeling, from the beginning, that Elliot Sanders was one of those heroes.

And then – and then – he had walked into the room, and she had laid eyes on him for the very first time.

He was taller, handsomer, more striking than she had ever begun to imagine he would be. It seemed that he sought her out from the very moment he set foot inside the dining room of his home – she could swear that his eyes, the same wide dark blue as those of his niece, had turned immediately in her direction.

Perhaps it was just wishful thinking…

But no. She knew better. She may have had a tendency to daydream, but there seemed no denying the fact that, again and again throughout that first dinner, she had caught him looking in her direction. She could scarcely meet his gaze; she'd never met a man as handsome, as strikingly self-possessed, as Elliot Sanders. Every time she even thought about glancing to her left to look at him, it seemed another blush would creep over her cheeks.

The knowledge that he was a good man made the attraction even more powerful.

Even now, some eleven days later, she couldn't entirely recall what had been discussed at that dinner. It had all been a whirlwind, a blur – a lovely, rose-tinted fantasy.

All she knew was that the few times he directly addressed her in the conversation, she had been unable to reply with much more than murmurs. And that certainly wasn't going to endear her to him. She railed at herself for such clumsiness. Especially in comparison to Lorna, who was bright and bubbly and vivacious. Lorna had eyes for no one but Curtis, but surely Elliot must have noted the marked difference between effervescent Lorna and shy, quiet Bell…

And that wasn't even the beginning of her troubles. Elliot was clearly a man who knew his own mind. What would he think when he found out she had come there as a Mail Order Bride at the behest of his own niece? Of course, it wasn't Bell's fault – but still, she was uncomfortably aware of the fact that, ultimately, she and Maria had conspired to keep something from him. As though they knew better, as though they had the right to make the decision…

Her own bad experience with just this situation made her reluctant to allow the charade to continue. But it was Maria's secret to tell, not hers, and as long as Elliot's niece felt it was necessary to leave him in the dark, she could not justify speaking up to tell him the truth. Although, Maria was still young—not an adult with adult reasoning…

Yet…

The longer he was in the dark, the greater the chance that he might decide she was worth his interest after all…

Selfishness was no small factor in what made her decide to keep mum.

Selfishness, and a flame of hope for the future that refused to be blown out.

In the meantime, as Christmas crept ever closer, she helped Maria and Lorna with sewing stockings to gift to the unfortunate ones in town, in between listening to Lorna rhapsodize about Curtis and assisting her with sewing lace on a million and one tiny, delicate items that Bell weren't entirely sure had a functional use, but which would certainly be pretty by the time they were done with them. It was on one such afternoon, head bent to such a task, that a sigh escaped her without her quite being aware of it.

Lorna, however, had surfaced from her love-induced sleep long enough to register her friend was not as happy as she was.

"Goodness, what a sigh. What's wrong, Bell? Can I help?"

Bell heaved another sigh.

"No, I don't think so. I don't think that anyone can."

"Well, that's a terribly morbid way to approach things," said Lorna practically. "Tell me what you're thinking of, my dear friend, and we will see what can be done. At the very least, it will make you feel better to have spoken to someone about it."

Bell eyed her with a faint smile. "Will it?"

"I promise it will," said Lorna stoutly. "Now, tell me all."

Bell put her sewing down in her lap with yet another sigh.

"It just occurred to me," she said, "that in the two weeks since I first came to Shadow Gulch, I've only seen my intended husband three times. And each of those times, he was clearly exhausted and scarcely paying me any attention. Furthermore, though I know he is my intended husband, he certainly doesn't – and I don't seem to be any closer to informing him of that fact than I was when I first arrived."

There was a moment of silence while Lorna clearly sought desperately for a positive answer to such a difficult question.

"Well," she said at last, "I suppose the way you have to look at it is that you're working on your relationship, even while he doesn't know. It's a bit of a conundrum, I do understand – but for what it's worth, I believe in my heart you made the right decision."

Bell sighed – again.

"I believe so, too," she said. "It's just that sometimes it sort of overwhelms me, the enormity of the decision I've made – and I start to wonder."

Lorna reached over and laid a hand on her shoulder, smiling in a comforting way.

"I know, my dear," she said. "But be patient, and trust that you will be rewarded for your good nature and pure spirit. From what you told me about Boston, it isn't as though you would be any better off if you had stayed."

"No, that's certainly true," Bell agreed. "I never met the man that Mr. Marin decided I should marry, but he certainly didn't sound as though he had any romance in his soul."

"I would say not. But Elliot Sanders, on the other hand – well, my dear, all I can say is I think he is worth waiting for."

Bell nodded and picked up her sewing again.

"You're right," she said with resolve. "I believe he is, too. I just need to give him some time – and let him get to know me."

"And when he does," Lorna said, "he won't be able to help but love you." She squeezed Bell's shoulder, and then picked up her own work again, setting to it with a will. "As we all do. In the meantime, has it occurred to you that I'm getting married in just a few days? Can you believe it? And to such a handsome man, to boot. I tell you, I can't quite believe my good fortune. I ought to send a thank you card to the matrimonial agency. Or perhaps just a Christmas card – a Christmas card with a photograph of our wedding."

And she was off again, gabbing cheerfully about Curtis this, Curtis that. Bell nodded, only halfway paying attention. She knew that her friend meant well and wanted the best for her. And she knew Elliot was a prize worth fighting to win.

Even if the fighting was just a matter of being patient.

But she couldn't help but wonder. What would happen if he did not grow to like her after all? What would happen if he was upset when he found out the truth?

Where would she be, come Christmas time?

# CHAPTER 9

Five days before Christmas, Elliot allowed Maria to straighten his tie, held his arm out to her to take, and led her out toward the church. It was three blocks away, a short walk on a warm summer's day, but a much longer one on a cold and wintry day in December. Tagging along behind them, the twins were shivering but enjoying the outing all the same.

He couldn't quite believe that his young friend was actually getting married – and to a woman he'd only known for the past few weeks, to boot. But all that being said, it was obvious that Curtis and Lorna were meant to be together. They were clearly infatuated with each other, but it was more than that. Lorna was friendly and conversational where Curtis was quiet and reserved; Curtis was level-headed and thoughtful where Lorna was apt to get distracted and act on impulse. It was a good match all around, and even Hannah approved of her older brother's decision.

And so, Elliot decided the best thing to do was again shelve his own reservations about Mail Order Brides, and simply support his friend as best as he knew how.

Which meant attending the wedding in style. He rarely had a chance to dress in his Sunday best – even on Sundays, he tended to put it off, feeling as though the suit required a truly special occasion – but Maria had suggested, he had demurred, and then she had insisted. And now here he was in his best suit, marching down the street to the church to stand up beside his friend, and with pretty little Maria on his arm and the twins also dressed to the nines, he couldn't have been prouder of his little family.

The whole town had turned out for the wedding, which was no surprise. Curtis was a popular young man, and there was little to do in the way of entertainment in Shadow Gulch through the cold winter months. Other than the upcoming Christmas festival, which was always a treat, this would be the only occasion for which the townsfolk felt it was worth it to get dressed up and go out in the cold.

Elliot was glad for his friend. There was nothing quite like the feeling of being lovingly supported by your entire town, especially on a day like this.

The church had been decorated with pine boughs and wreaths, filling it with the clean scent of winter. Elliot made his way up to the front to stand beside Curtis, who was blushing off and on as though his internal fires were being alternately stoked and banked. He, too, was dressed in his Sunday best, and looked just as uncomfortable as Elliot felt.

Elliot nudged his friend in the ribs.

"Today's the day."

"I feel as though it's been forever," Curtis said out of the side of his mouth. "And yet, somehow, it all passed by in the blink of an eye. Tell me I'm not dreaming."

Elliot smiled.

"You're not dreaming," he said.

The double doors opened, admitting the bride herself. Though the weather outside was wintry and cold, she entered looking like the centerpiece of a summer wedding cake, sure of her steps and beautiful as the spring. Lorna Olsen had proclaimed to one and all that she had awaited this day for longer than she'd even known Curtis Lockhart, and her overflowing joy was obvious as she proceeded down the aisle. But Elliot wasn't looking at Lorna Olsen.

He was looking at the young woman who preceded her.

Lorna had asked both Hannah and Bell to be her attendants, and the two had consented readily. Their dresses were made over from old clothing they already owned, but with the addition of lace and careful fittings, each dress fit like a glove, and each girl shone with a light of her own as she walked down before the bride. It occurred to Elliot that this was the first wedding he'd ever attended in which he felt that the beauty of the procedure was truly exemplified in the people involved. Between Lorna, Hannah, and Bell, it was difficult to imagine a more perfect trio to embody the spirit of a Christmas wedding.

And of the three of them, it was impossible for him to deny Bell was the most beautiful.

With her unusual looks, she was far more attractive than any woman he'd ever seen. He'd thought that from the very first day he met her, and the thought leapt unbidden to his mind now.

The most irksome thing, of course, was that once the thought entered his mind, it seemed impossible to get rid of it.

He tried to focus on the words of the minister. He tried to focus on the joy on his friend's face as he repeated his vows. He even tried, Lord help him, to think of how painful it had been when Cordelia had left him flat and broken their engagement.

But all he could think of, as the wedding ceremony was carried out, was how beautiful Bell Wade really was.

And she caught him looking, which was truly horrible. He could tell by the blush that stole over her cheeks as the vows were being said, and the way in which she carefully avoided meeting his gaze.

On the whole, he felt terrible about it. Terrible, and rather embarrassed. After all, the poor girl certainly hadn't asked for him to pay her any attention, or to stare. It wasn't as though she had come out here to be *his* Mail Order Bride.

Like it or not, Bell Wade occupied his thoughts for the rest of the ceremony, to the point where he was half dazed to realize the happy couple were now truly husband and wife. He shook hands with Curtis, kissed Lorna on the cheek dutifully, and reflected that he was now, at last, released from duty. He no longer had to suffer through the tumult in his mind.

His relief was short lived, as Maria informed him, beaming, that his presence was expected at the town hall for the wedding reception.

He couldn't help himself. He clapped a hand to his forehead and groaned.

"Oh, Maria, do I really have to go?"

She folded her arms.

"I'm afraid so, Uncle. Everyone will talk if you don't show your face for at least three dances – and at least half of them will still talk if you don't stay for five."

"Do we care about whether they talk or not?"

Now she had her hands on her hips, which was far worse. He closed his eyes.

"Uncle," she said, severely, "you know how important you are in town. The good folks here count on you. If you don't come to the party and show them how it's done, they won't know how to enjoy themselves."

Elliot cracked one eye open, enough to see that she was smiling at him. She was teasing, that much was evident – but she meant it, all the same, and he knew it in his heart.

"Very well," he said. "I suppose since I'm already dressed for the occasion..."

The town hall was, if possible, even more extravagantly bedecked with the trappings of a celebratory Christmas event, with pine boughs liberally spread everywhere and candles carefully arranged. It had the effect of a dazzling winter wonderland, and he couldn't deny the impact it had on him – as well as, more importantly, the impact it had on the twins. He called after them to stay away from the flickering flames as they scampered off, calling to each other about finding the source of Christmas.

Maria, standing beside him, grinned at him with a teasing note she did not often show but which seemed to be quite evident tonight.

"Now that you're here," she said, "I suppose I should tell you that you must find someone to dance with."

"Maria, you know I'm a terrible dancer."

"No," she said truthfully. "I know you've always told me that you're a terrible dancer, but I've never seen you dance at all. I suppose you'll just have to prove it to me, and then I promise never to ask you again."

Elliot sighed. He thought briefly, longingly, of his practice, packed with patients during the day – what he wouldn't give to be back there, with a host of sick townsfolk waiting on him. But he knew the office was empty; the townsfolk were all here, sickly or not. And he had no choice but to dance.

The only question was – with whom?

At the very least, Maria did not offer to choose someone for him. He was grateful for that. Perhaps he wasn't the most decisive man on the planet, but at the very least he did not need his young niece to choose a dancing partner.

He could ask Mrs. Adams – she wouldn't mind.

Mrs. MacGill, too, her husband was notorious for refusing to dance, and she was safely of dowager age and would case no raised eyebrows.

As far as dancing with an unmarried woman, the only one he could think of was…

…Bell Wade.

The thought had been there all along. He simply had refused to acknowledge it. She entered the town hall at that very moment, and he was struck anew by her beauty. She was mesmerizing, and he was caught and trapped – before he knew it, he was standing in front of her, and she was looking up at him with those big eyes, catching her breath.

He heard his own voice as though it belonged to a stranger. "Will you dance with me, Miss Wade?"

Her long black eyelashes dropped swiftly, but he heard her say, "Yes, Doc Sanders, I will."

Then they were dancing, and she was in his arms, and he had no clear idea of how they had gotten to this position, or what had happened along the way. All he knew was the most beautiful girl he'd ever seen, the one he couldn't seem to chase from his thoughts over the last two weeks, was right there, warm underneath his grasp, and when she finally looked up to meet his gaze, he saw he was not the only one who was affected by their proximity.

The tune was nearly over when she took a deep breath and said, her voice half strangled, "I must get some air."

Elliot looked up and around. The rest of the town was either dancing alongside them or standing in a ring around the dancing floor. The newly married couple was sitting on a small settee at the top of the room, each with a small goblet of port wine in hand. They were surrounded by cheerful festivities and lots of noise, and no one would notice if he left the hall.

He took Bell by the hand and led her swiftly toward the door.

They stepped outside into the frigid night air. The clouds of earlier in the day had cleared, leaving a sheet of frosty stars overlaying the entire town. The lights inside the hall blazed merrily, and the beat and pulse of the music from within chased away the coldness of the outdoors.

Bell stepped away from him, though she did not relinquish his grasp. She turned to the darkness outside and took in a deep breath.

"I can hardly believe it," she said.

Elliot, half dazed and not really sure what she meant, nevertheless knew the sentiment. It echoed to something deep within him. "Neither can I."

"Doc Sanders," she said, turning back in his direction but not looking at him, "there's something that I must tell you…"

"Please – call me Elliot."

Almost as though it was against her will, her eyes fluttered upward and met his.

"Elliot," she whispered.

He could stand it no longer. Though his mind was screaming wildly at him that women were not to be trusted, that he would only end up hurt yet again, that he could not make a poorer decision, that he hardly knew the girl, he was stepping closer and gathering her up in his arms. With the diamond stars above, in the cold winter's night, she went willingly and turned her face upward to his. He kissed her in the dark, with the warmth and noise of the wedding party on one side and the cold of the winter on the other.

And then the terrified yelling in his head overwhelmed the thoughts of embracing her, and he drew back, eyes wide.

He hardly knew her – knew only that he was drawn to her as he had never been drawn to anyone.

But that in itself wasn't enough.

He had no idea if he could trust her. There was too much at stake. He owed it to his nieces and nephew to keep his heart cold and aloof, to refrain from ever letting them be hurt again. Any of them…

She was looking up at him with such trust in her eyes…

But he swallowed hard and clenched his jaw and let her go.

"I'm sorry," he said abruptly. "That was very – ungentlemanly of me. I'm…I'm sorry."

There was nothing else to say, nothing that would take away the heartbreak he saw in her eyes. But he had felt that same heartbreak. He knew it of old.

He touched his hat with a misplaced politeness.

"Good night, Miss Wade," he said, and he left her there.

# CHAPTER 10

Two days before Christmas, Bell Wade could not stop thinking about Elliot Sanders.

Or, to be more specific, about the kiss the two of them had shared after the wedding of Curtis and Lorna.

He had seemed so sure of himself, so definite in his desire as he swept her up into his arms. And then – and then – everything had changed. Changed so swiftly and completely that she was left wondering whether he was even the same man. A remote coldness had descended over his face, the distance of someone caught up in a memory. She wasn't even entirely certain he was still seeing her before him; at least, not until he said her name.

*Good night, Miss Wade*, he had said.

*That was very ungentlemanly of me. I'm sorry. Good night.*

Well, *she* wasn't sorry. Shouldn't he have asked her how *she* felt about it?

She spent the next day at the ranch with Hannah, since Lorna and Curtis had gone to Lewiston for a two-day honeymoon, ranting and raving inside the safety of her own head. From the moment she had met Elliot Sanders, she had dreamed about him, built a love for him. He was everything she wanted and more, and she was foolish enough to think Maria's plan to get them together would somehow work out after all.

And the night of the wedding, she had thought for one brief moment that perhaps it would all come together as it was meant to right then—that night. A Christmas miracle, like meeting Lorna on the train.

But now…

Now, she was no longer so sure. She no longer knew what to expect from him. He was still high in her esteem, but her spirit was crushed, and she couldn't deny it.

Elliot Sanders had proven to be both more and less than she had expected. And there seemed to be nothing she could do about it.

If only she could tell him the truth. She had been thinking of it endlessly, especially in the moments before he kissed her. It occurred to her that, somehow, she really believed if she had just been honest with him, he wouldn't have changed his mind after the kiss. He would have stuck it out. He would have changed his mind. It didn't make any sense, and she knew it, but it was what she believed all the same.

There was nothing to be done about it now – nothing but stew.

And stewing was precisely what she was doing when she said goodbye to Hannah the next morning and went to visit Maria.

Between the group of them – Hannah, Maria, Lorna, and Bell – they had been sewing Christmas stockings for all the needy children in town. Maria was keeping them at their house, as they lived right in town and could collect extra materials from donations. With only a few days until Christmas, it was certainly time that the last few stockings that had been finished were distributed to the deserving children of Shadow Gulch. With the finished stockings wrapped up in brown paper and tucked under her arm, Bell set out to deliver them to Maria – and have a bit of a chat.

Perhaps it was the extent to which she had been stewing on the matter that made her speak. Or perhaps it was because of how high her hopes had flown when Elliot kissed her – and how badly they had been crushed when he stepped away from her, cold and remote as the moon. Whatever the cause, it wasn't more than ten minutes into her visit with Maria that she burst out, "I believe that your uncle needs to know the truth."

Maria was stirring a pot of cranberries on the stove, turning them slowly but surely into the thick jam-like preserves for which she was already deservedly famous in Shadow Gulch. She turned a look of surprise on Bell, her eyebrows raised.

"The truth?"

"Yes," said Bell shortly. "The truth about how you wrote to me as a Mail Order Bride, to come out here and marry your uncle. That truth."

"Oh, Bell," said Maria softly. "I don't think it's time yet…"

"But I do. I don't think you understand, Maria – you're still so young, and Elliot is obviously raising you very well. But it's a terrible thing to have someone decide your life for you. I understand – someone tried to do the same thing to me." She pressed the heel of her hand to her forehead, wincing at the memory. "That's how I ended up here, as a matter of fact. I don't want anyone to decide for me…"

"But Bell," said Maria, setting the spoon down and turning to her, "if you could only understand – Uncle Elliot might say no. He seems to just carry on as though he'll never know love again, as though that's the decision that he made when he agreed to take us on, and Cordelia left him. It's almost as though it's a… a punishment. A punishment that he deserves for being a good man. But he doesn't deserve any punishment…"

"I agree," said Bell, sighing heavily. "He is a good man. And I want what is best for him. But Maria, you are only fifteen, after all – do you really think that you know what's best for your uncle?"

Maria's eyes were full of trust and faith.

"Yes," she said simply. "Yes, I do. I believe you are best for my uncle. That's why I wrote the letter to the agency. And if you'll only trust me, and stick by me, then I believe that we will give him enough time to understand…and come to love you as everyone does." There was a lengthy pause broken only by the soft bubbling sounds from the pot on the stovetop. "Will you wait, Bell? Wait, and hold off on telling him the truth a little bit longer?"

Bell took a deep breath and let it out slowly. "Yes," she said, "I suppose I will."

"That's all I needed to hear," said a voice from the hallway.

Bell's stomach dropped somewhere to the vicinity of her toes, while her heart beat ever faster. She saw, in a blur, that Maria's face was as shocked as her own must be. Elliot Sanders had stepped out of the hallway and into the light of the kitchen. His face was the color of ash, and he looked first to his niece.

"I can't believe you would betray me like this," he said simply, and his words had the impact of stones being thrown. "You ought to know better, Maria."

Maria's eyes filled with tears, and Bell jumped in, unable to stand by and watch the young woman being upset in this way.

"You don't understand, Elliot…"

"And you." His eyes turned to her, and she felt as though she was being cut in half with the sharpness of his gaze. "She's just a little girl, but you – you're a grown woman. What sort of example are you setting, leading her on like this, encouraging her to lie to her guardian?"

The look on his face was hurt, cold, remote – as though her betrayal had meant just as much as that of his niece. Bell swallowed.

"Elliot…" she started/

"I'll ask you to kindly leave my house, Miss Wade. Now, please."

As he spoke, he returned his stern gaze to his niece, who looked like a butterfly suddenly pinned down in a collection. But Bell's heart was in her throat, and she had never felt this bereft – not since her father had died. With his gaze turned from her, as cold as it had been, she understood suddenly that she had fallen in love with Elliot Sanders. And with his love removed from her, she had no reason to be here in Shadow Gulch.

She had no reason to be anywhere.

She had time just enough to gasp, "I'm sorry," as she rushed for the door.

Then she was outside, and the cold settled into her bones.

# CHAPTER 11

The clouds had made good on their threats. The snow had begun at last to fall, thick and soft as a velvet blanket on the landscape of Shadow Gulch.

It would be a white Christmas after all.

Bell had rushed away without her coat. She could not go back; she could not face up to seeing the disappointment and betrayal and rejection in Elliot's eyes once more. She had no choice but to struggle on – and hope that she made it back to the Lockhart ranch before she got too cold.

But already the snow was thick, and her vision was impaired. She could not see more than a few feet in front of her.

A white Christmas – a Christmas miracle – her mind went over and over the facts, thinking of her hope, and thinking of how quickly her hope had been dashed.

She had fallen in love with Elliot Sanders…but he had not fallen in love with her. She had agreed to marry Elliot Sanders, but he had not agreed to marry her. Everything she had chosen to do, the plan she had made, had fallen through.

Perhaps she should have stayed in Boston. Perhaps Hank Marin had known best…

She choked back a sob as she pressed onward, hoping that she was still going in the right direction. It was impossible to think someone else's decision for her life was the right one, and everything she had tried to do was only wrong, wrong, wrong.

But she had no proof her decisions were right. On the contrary, she had only proof they were a fallacy. She had tried to be a Mail Order Bride and had contracted with the niece of the man she'd agreed to marry. She had befriended Lorna and become irritated at their friendship as Lorna's life ascended into bliss and her own descended into frustration. She had fallen in love with a man who had told her in no uncertain terms to leave, even though he had been attracted enough to her to kiss her…

She wondered if her tears were frozen. She certainly didn't seem to be able to see clearly, and there was no warmth on her cheeks. She didn't recognize where she was; the snow had covered everything, obscuring landmarks.

She had nowhere to go. Not even back to Boston.

Stumbling slightly over her next steps, her exhaustion caught up with her – more mental than physical, but real nonetheless. Before she knew it, she was slumped in the snow, shivering. The snowflakes fell and caught on her lashes, but she was conscious of a curious warmth. It was as though the sun had suddenly come out to warm her…

She wondered vaguely if she would be found like this – if Elliot would try to revive her – or if he would stand stoically by and let her slip into oblivion. It was a just and righteous end to her sad little misadventure. Hank Marin would be pleased…

She didn't know how long she lay there in the peaceful snow, but eventually she was conscious of sounds in the distance.

The sounds went on for some time, and then resolved into words.

"I found her."

Then there was a fuss, and she was surrounded by familiar faces. Maria, Curtis, even Lorna – they must have just gotten back from their honeymoon, though it scarcely seemed as though it could have been two days since the wedding. She thought she heard the twins in the distance. And then, impossibly, Elliot's handsome face was hovering over her, and Elliot's calm, comforting voice was giving instructions. She should be handled carefully. Someone should bring a blanket. He must make sure that nothing was broken from the fall.

"I didn't fall," she protested, but she knew it wasn't entirely true. She had fallen – if not into the snow, then into love with Elliot. Her mind was chilled and frozen enough that the two things seemed synonymous, as though she couldn't have one without the other.

Elliot put a warm hand on her forehead, soothing her.

"I know, my darling," he whispered. "I know."

Then Elliot's strong arms were around her, and he was lifting her as though she weighed no more than a feather. She curled into him, creeping one hand up and around his neck.

"This is…hypothermia," she whispered. "I believe I'm dreaming."

Elliot puffed out a laugh.

"This is more than likely hypothermia," he said, "though I'll have to get you into my office for examination before I can be certain. We're taking you home for now, however. That can wait."

"Home?"

He looked down at her and smiled.

"Home," he said. "My home. So I can keep an eye on you. I hope you don't object."

She wouldn't have objected even if she could. She'd never known bliss quite like this.

"Thought … you didn't want me under … your roof," she whispered.

She could have been mistaken, but she was relatively sure his expression turned embarrassed.

"Maria explained it all to me," he said. "I'm sorry I was so harsh. It wasn't your fault at all – and Maria only did what she did out of good intentions. I don't agree with what she did, but I can't fault her for why she did it. Besides." He coughed. "I can't exactly argue with her methods when things turned out as she expected, can I?"

Bell looked up at him as though through a fine mist. "What do you mean?"

"Well – I mean – she wanted me to find love again, to trust again. And as much as I cannot condone her methods…it worked."

Bell struggled to sit up. Since she was still in his arms, she had mixed results.

"It worked?"

"It did."

"Tell me – tell me what that means."

Elliot trudging determinedly through the snow and into his home before once again giving her his full attention.

"It means," he said, "that though I had no intention of ever being married, and certainly not to a Mail Order Bride, it turns out that I actually am quite drawn to this young woman that I met recently – a certain Bellissima Wade – of Italian descent, I assume – and I can't quite seem to get her out of my thoughts. Perhaps you've heard of her?"

She wanted so badly to kiss him, but she knew that her lips would be terribly cold. So she hid her face against his shoulder instead.

"Do you know what I tried to tell myself?" she whispered. "Back in Boston, when everyone was making decisions for me? 'Better the silence and a roof over your head than happiness in the cold.'"

The movements of his hands over her arms, stroking, building the warmth little by little, were a blessing to her soul.

"Do you still believe that?" he asked quietly.

She looked up at him, her whole heart in her eyes.

"Give me the cold any day," she said. "After all, it's almost Christmas."

"That it is," he said with a smile. "You will marry me, won't you, dear Bell?"

"I will," she said, still feeling in somewhat of a daze.

"Engaged by Christmas," he said, leaning down to tenderly kiss her forehead.

The End

CONTINUE READING...

Thank you for reading *Engaged by Christmas!* Are you wondering **what to read next?** Why not read *Christmas at the Inn?* **Here's a peek for you:**

The day that Rebecca Vanderhall learned of her inevitable fate dawned cold and bright. The brilliant sunlight and the achingly clear blue skies were a stark contrast to the darkness of the future that she now knew awaited her.

Her father, seated at the head of the table and wearing his usual three-piece suit and thunderous scowl, relayed the news to her with utmost calm.

She would have expected nothing less from him.

Still, his pronouncement felt like a slap to the face as she was faced with the reality, the unchangeableness of his words.

Numbly, she repeated his words. "I'm to marry – and I am betrothed to Mr. Reginald Rogers."

Vaughn Vanderhall gave a single nod. She should not push her luck any further; her father did not appreciate being questioned. But she couldn't quite keep herself from speaking out once more.

"But Father, I don't want to marry him."

His brows drew down even further over his hawklike nose. "Why not, pray tell? Have you something against the holy arrangement of matrimony?"

"Well, no," she managed. Truthfully, she had often secretly dreamed of marrying someone – preferably someone who lived thousands of miles away, someone who swept her off her feet and carried her off into the sunset without so much as asking permission to court her – or a second glance.

"Then what could possibly be your objection? He's a fine, upstanding young man. You know he is my particular protégé – when I look at that young man, I see myself, thirty years ago."

Becky bit her lip. That was exactly the problem; Reginald Rogers was the spitting image of her father. The idea of being tied to him for life was enough to make her cry.

But she couldn't cry here, not in front of her father, who was taking her silence as a sign that her objection had been forcefully overcome.

As well he might. Becky was an unmarried woman of twenty-one, still living under her father's roof, and in the eyes of society, he had every right to make arrangements for her marriage. In theory, a marriage was to provide for her care and keeping; thinking of what Rogers might be like as a husband, on the other hand, gave her the shudders.

**Visit HERE To Read More!**

https://ticahousepublishing.com/mail-order-brides.html

# ABOUT THE AUTHOR

Susannah has always been intrigued with the Western movement - prairie days, mail-order brides, the gold rush, frontier life! As a writer, she's excited to combine her love of story with her love of all that is Western. Presently, Susannah lives in Wyoming with her hubby and their three amazing children.

www.ticahousepublishing.com
contact@ticahousepublishing.com